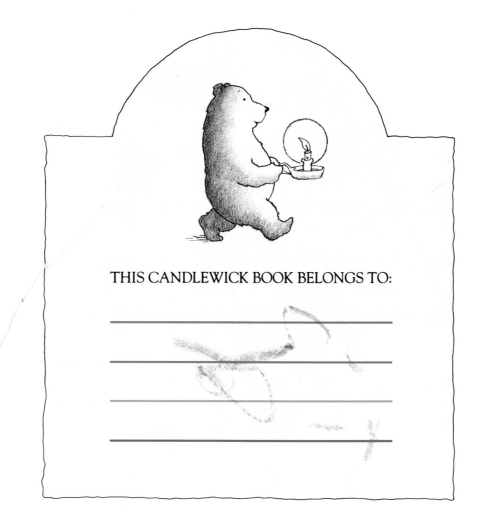

THIS CANDLEWICK BOOK BELONGS TO:

_____

_____

_____

_____

For Oscar

Copyright © 1994 by Catherine and Laurence Anholt

All rights reserved.

First U.S. paperback edition 1996

The Library of Congress has cataloged the hardcover edition as follows:

Anholt, Catherine.
What makes me happy? / by Catherine and Laurence Anholt.—1st U.S. ed.
Summary: Children describe in rhyming verse their feelings and what makes them feel different ways.
ISBN 1-56402-482-2 (hardcover)
[1. Emotions—Fiction.   2. Stories in rhyme.]   I. Anholt, Laurence.   II. Title.
PZ8.3.A5492Wj   1995
[E]—dc20   94-5144

ISBN 1-56402-828-3 (paperback)

4 6 8 10 9 7 5 3

Printed in Hong Kong

This book was typeset in M Bembo.
The pictures were done in ink and watercolor.

Candlewick Press
2067 Massachusetts Avenue
Cambridge, Massachusetts 02140

What Makes Me Happy?

Catherine and Laurence Anholt

CANDLEWICK PRESS

CAMBRIDGE, MASSACHUSETTS

What makes me laugh?

tickly toes

a big red nose

being rude

silly food

acting crazy

my friend Maisie

What makes me cry?

wasps that sting

a fall from a swing

wobbly wheels

head over heels

What makes me bored?

Grown-ups . . .

moaning groaning eating meeting walking talking

feeding reading sitting knitting stopping shopping

What makes me proud?

Look how much I've grown!

I can do it on my own!

What makes me jealous?

Her!

What makes me scared?

shrieks

creaks

jaws

claws

bangs

gangs

caves

waves

What makes me sad?

Rain, rain, every day.

No one wants to let me play.

Someone special's far away.

What makes us excited?

a roller coaster ride

Here comes the bride!

The monster's on his way!

a special party day

What makes me shy?

My first day.

What makes me mad?

Days when buttons won't go straight
and I want to stay up late
and I hate what's on my plate . . .
Why won't anybody wait?

What makes us all happy?

playing in the sun

a box full of fun

singing a song

skipping along

windy weather

finding a feather, and . . .

being together.

CATHERINE **and** LAURENCE ANHOLT met while attending art school. They have since collaborated on more than twenty books for children, including *Kids, Here Come the Babies, The Twins Two by Two,* and *Come Back, Jack!* They created *What Makes Me Happy?* to help children explore their own emotions. The Anholts are the parents of three children, including twins.